Yaffle's Journey

Nancy Keating

Illustrated by Laurel Keating and Nancy Keating

We gratefully acknowledge the financial support of the Canada Council for the Arts, the Government of Canada through the Canada Book Fund (CBF), and the Government of Newfoundland and Labrador through the Department of Tourism, Culture and Recreation for our publishing program.

Illustrations and book design © 2013, Nancy Keating and Laurel Keating
Cover and inside layout © 2013, Todd Manning

Published by
TUCKAMORE BOOKS
an imprint of CREATIVE BOOK PUBLISHING
a Transcontinental Inc. associated company
P.O. Box 8660, St. John's,
Newfoundland and Labrador
A1B 3T7

Printed in Canada by:
Transcontinental Inc.

Printed on acid-free paper

Library and Archives Canada Cataloguing in Publication

Keating, Nancy
    Yaffle's journey / Nancy Keating & Laurel Keating.

ISBN 978-1-77103-007-6

    I. Keating, Laurel, 1990- II. Title.

PS8621.E2348Y24 2013   jC813'.6   C2013-900511-0

Yaffle's Journey

Nancy Keating

Illustrated by Laurel Keating and Nancy Keating

Tuckamore Books
a Creative Publishers imprint

St. John's, Newfoundland and Labrador
2013

On the ninth day of rain in a row,
Yaffle said, "This has to go;
I've had it to here with bad weather all year,
And the rain, drizzle, fog, and wet snow."

"So I'm heading south, yes today!"
He declared as the fog filled the bay.
"This place is too stormy; I'll go someplace warm-y,
'Cause I just can't live in this way."

If he left Newfoundland, Yaffle knew,
He'd be leaving his friends behind too,
And his nook in the rock and his perch on the dock.
The thought of it made Yaffle blue.

So Yaffle sat down and he thought.
And soon he had hatched up a plot.
"I won't leave behind all the things that are mine;
I'll take them and run with the lot."

"I'll bet this here island can float,
And got stuck up here, wet and remote.
I'll just pull it all free from this mauzy old sea,
And tow it down south like a boat."

His heart filling up with new hope,
Yaffle came out of his mope.
He'd drag Newfoundland to sunny, warm sands;
He tied up the wharf with a rope.

With the rope in his beak, Yaffle soared
As the drizzling rain ceaselessly poured.
At a very great height, he tugged with his might,
While the ocean below Yaffle roared.

It was hard, heavy work and so slow,
But a helpful wind started to blow.
He got tired, he got hot, but he pulled, and he fought
Till Newfoundland finally let go.

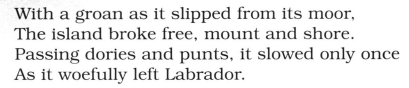

With a groan as it slipped from its moor,
The island broke free, mount and shore.
Passing dories and punts, it slowed only once
As it woefully left Labrador.

The hard work behind him all done,
With the prospect of cloudless, warm fun,
And a smile on his beak (not one final peek),
Yaffle set off for the sun.

"It won't be long now," Yaffle said,
As he followed where warm breezes led.
In a week and a half, with a triumphant laugh,
He said, "I can see palm trees ahead!"

With the sight of a warm, welcome beach,
Just a hop, skip, and jump from his reach,
At a sandy white slope, he pulled back the rope,
And came to a halt with a screech.

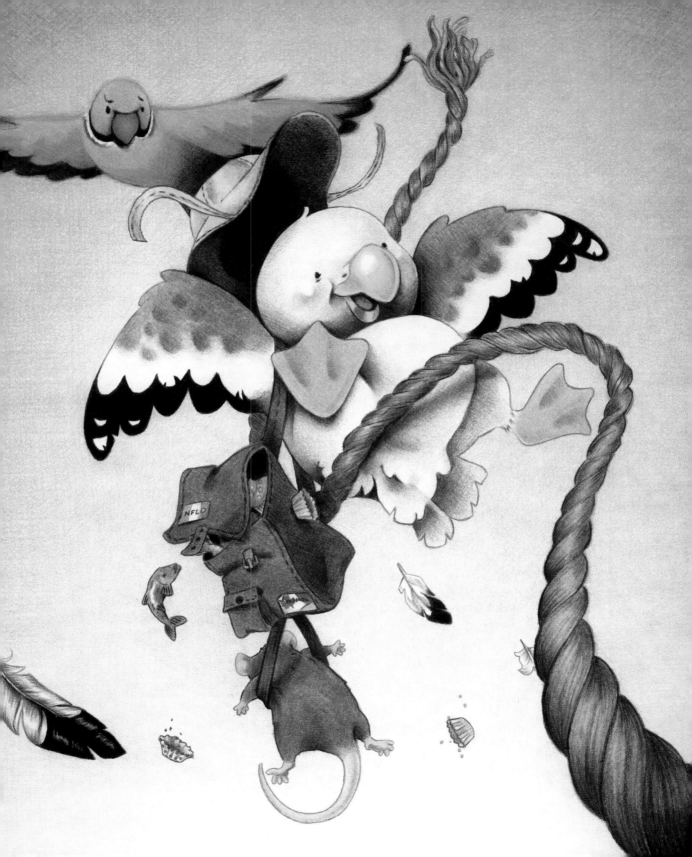

"Wait," he thought, "this isn't good."
For the sun didn't shine as it should.
He puzzled aloud of the heavy grey cloud
That hung overhead like a hood.

It didn't take Yaffle too long
To understand what had gone wrong.
Unlike he had planned, when he'd towed Newfoundland,
The weather had followed along!

Like a lightning bolt from high above,
Something hit him he'd never thought of.
And he knew in his heart, the bad weather was part
Of the place that he knew and he loved.

And Yaffle could suddenly see,
As he welcomed his true destiny,
He could carp and complain of fog, drizzle, and rain,
But some things are just meant to be.

So Yaffle now knew: All along,
His attitude had been all wrong.
He'd tow Newfoundland to right where he began,
And put it back where it belonged.

So both Newfoundland and he
Came home from their trek on the sea.
Yaffle's story now ends as he flocks to his friends,
'Cause some things are just meant to be.